The Fright
Before Christmas

The Fright
Before Christmas

by **James Howe**

illustrated by **Jeff Mack**

Atheneum Books for Young Readers

New York   London   Toronto   Sydney

Atheneum Books for Young Readers
An imprint of Simon & Schuster Children's Publishing Division
1230 Avenue of the Americas, New York, New York 10020
Book design by Michael McCartney
The text for this book is set in Century Old Style.
The illustrations for this book are rendered in acrylic.
Manufactured in the United States of America
First Edition
10 9 8 7 6 5 4 3 2 1
Library of Congress Cataloging-in-Publication Data
Howe, James, 1946–
The fright before Christmas / James Howe ; illustrated by Jeff
Mack.—1st ed.
p. cm. — (Bunnicula and friends; #5)
Summary: Howie the dog is afraid of Santa Claus and believes ghosts
are haunting Christmas.
ISBN-13: 978-0-689-86939-6
ISBN-10: 0-689-86939-8
[1. Christmas—Fiction. 2. Santa Claus—Fiction. 3. Ghosts—Fiction.]
I. Mack, Jeff, ill. II. Title. III. Series.
PZ7.H83727Fri 2006
[Fic]—dc22
2005011627

CHAPTER 1:

A Scary Christmas

It was Christmas Eve at the Monroes' house. And Howie was scared.

"What do you mean a big fat man in a red suit is going to come down the chimney?" he cried. "What does he want?"

"He doesn't want anything," I explained. "He has this bag he carries over his shoulder and—"

Howie ran out of the room before I could finish my sentence.

"Why do you think Howie is so afraid of Santa Claus?" I asked Chester.

Chester didn't answer. He was rolling around under the Christmas tree with a piece of ribbon, playing cute.

Chester always tries to get in a little extra cuteness the day before Christmas. He thinks he'll get more presents that way.

"You can drop the act," I said. "Nobody's here. And you certainly don't have to play cute for me."

Chester glanced around and dropped the ribbon.

"Now what is this about Howie being scared?" he asked.

"Howie seems to be scared of Santa Claus," I said.

"Scared of Santa Claus?" Chester cried. "Who would be scared of Santa Claus?"

"Beats me. But he's sure scared of something."

"Maybe he's scared of the ghosts," Chester said.

"Ghosts?" I took a good look at Chester. Maybe all that cuteness had gone to his head. "This is Christmas, not Halloween."

"Yes, I know," Chester sniffed. "But there are ghosts all the same."

Now there's something I should tell you about Chester. He's a cat with a big imagination. I think it comes from all the mystery books he reads.

"Don't you remember that story
Mr. Monroe read to Toby and Pete
last night?" Chester asked.

"The one about the stingy old man
and the poor little boy?" I said.

"Exactly!" Chester cried. "There
were ghosts in that story. They
walked through walls and rattled
their chains."

"Thanks for reminding me," I said.

"And when did those ghosts appear?" Chester asked.

I thought for a minute. "On Christmas Eve?"

"That's right!" Chester cried. "No wonder Howie is afraid."

And no wonder I had a hard time falling asleep that night. It's never easy to fall asleep the night before Christmas, but when you have ghosts to worry about it's almost impossible.

CHAPTER 2:

Strange Noises

It took a lot of staring out the kitchen window, counting snowflakes, but finally I did it. I fell asleep.

I was having a perfectly yummy dream when something—or someone—woke me up again.

It was Chester, of course.

"This had better be good," I said. "I was just about to eat an entire plate of Christmas cookies."

"By yourself?" Chester asked.

I nodded.

"You weren't going to share?"

"No."

"Then maybe I won't tell you about the strange noises," Chester sniffed.

"Fine by me," I said, and tried to go back to my dream.

"Well, don't you hear them?"
Chester asked.

I sighed. "Hear what?"

"Those noises!" Chester cried.
"There's a ghost in this house, I just
know it!"

"Shhh!" I said. "I don't want you
waking up poor Howie and scaring
him all over again."

I closed my eyes. Then I opened them.

Now I could hear the strange noises.

Something *was* moving around
somewhere in the house. It wasn't
Howie. He seemed to be sound
asleep under his blanket.

"Follow me!" Chester said.

I didn't really want to follow him, but I knew I had no choice. Chester would never let me go back to sleep now.

Quietly, we crept up the stairs.

First we checked Mr. and Mrs.
Monroe's room.

"No strange noises here," Chester
announced.

"Unless you count Mr. Monroe's
snoring," I said.

Next we went to Toby's room.
"No ghosts here," I said with relief.
Toby is my favorite Monroe. He
lets me sleep in his bed and he
shares his snacks with me.

Finally we came to Pete's room.

He was asleep with his hands rolled into fists as if he were ready for a fight.

Pete's that kind of kid.

But he didn't look like he'd been fighting any ghosts.

"I guess all the ghosts have gone to bed," I said, yawning. "And that's exactly where we should be—in bed."

"I guess you're right," Chester said with a sigh.

We headed back downstairs.

When we got to the living room, we heard a soft rustling sound.

It was Bunnicula. He was moving around inside his cage.

"That rabbit!" Chester cried. "I should have known!"

Now there's something I should tell you about this rabbit of ours. He is a vampire bunny—or at least that's what Chester says.

Don't get too excited. Bunnicula only attacks vegetables.

Still, Chester is always ready to blame the little guy for anything strange that happens around here. And believe me, a lot of strange things happen around here.

Like the two of us looking for ghosts in the middle of the night. This kind of thing happens all the time. I should be used to it. But I'm not.

So when there was suddenly a loud CRASH, I knew something strange was going on. And I knew Chester wanted to blame Bunnicula, but he couldn't.

After all, Bunnicula was lying right in front of us, inside his cage. And the loud CRASH had definitely come from the cellar.

CHAPTER 3:

The Cellar

"All this time we've been looking for ghosts in the wrong places, Harold!" Chester cried.

"That's too bad," I said.

"In the story, one of the ghosts came up from the cellar," Chester continued. "Remember the rattling chains?"

"How could I forget?" I answered.

Chester rushed toward the cellar door.

I stayed right where I was.

"Let's go, Harold!" Chester cried. "We've got to get to the bottom of this!"

"Do we have to?" I sighed, but I already knew the answer.

Downstairs, the cellar was dark. And quiet.

"Nobody here," I said.

"Except our ghost," Chester hissed. "Don't you see it?"

"I don't see anything," I replied.

"Harold, it would help if you opened your eyes!" Chester said.

I opened one eye, and then the other.

Right away I wished I hadn't.

There, not five feet in front of us, was—

THE GHOST!

Before I could think of what to do,
Chester went wild. I had never seen
him so fierce. He was like a tiger.
He jumped up.
And the ghost fell down.
Right on top of me.

"Hey, this is no ghost!" I exclaimed.
"It's Mr. Monroe's Santa Claus
costume!"

Chester seemed disappointed, but I
was glad.

"I have an idea," I said.

"Will your idea help us catch our
ghost?" Chester asked hopefully.

"Well, no," I admitted, but I told him
anyway. "I'll wear this costume upstairs
and pretend to be Santa Claus."

"Now who's trying to play cute?"
Chester said.

"It's not for the Monroes. It's for
Howie," I replied.

Chester looked at me as if I had a
screw loose.

"When Howie wakes up and sees a
friendly Santa—his old Uncle Harold—
he won't be scared anymore!"
I explained.

"*If* it was Santa Claus he was scared of in the first place," muttered Chester.

It wasn't easy getting into the Santa suit. I only had half of it on when I heard someone breathing. And it didn't sound like Chester.

"Do ghosts breathe?" I asked, although I wasn't sure I wanted to know the answer.

CHAPTER 4:

The Ghost

The breathing was coming from a dark corner, behind a pile of junk.

"Come out, ghost! Show yourself!" Chester yelled.

All at once, the breathing stopped.

Then something moved.

It was the scariest, most horrible—

"Howie!" Chester cried. "What are you doing down here?"

"I was trying to hide from Santa Claus," Howie answered.

"*You* were making all the noise!" said Chester. "We thought you were asleep."

"I bunched up my blanket," Howie said. "I wanted to be sure that when Santa came, nobody would know where to find me."

"So *you're* our Christmas ghost," I said, stepping out from the shadows.

"Santa!" Howie yelped.

He streaked past me and smacked
right into a lamp.
Down it came with a CRASH!
The lampshade landed right on
Howie's head, but he kept going—
straight for the staircase.

Then a new sound stopped Howie in his tracks.

It was the floorboards above us.

They creaked.

They squeaked.

The doorknob began to rattle and turn. . . .

"H-help!" Howie yipped.

"Ghosts!" Chester gulped.

The door at the top of the stairs flew open with a bang.

Howie started to howl.

Chester hissed.

And Mrs. Monroe turned on the cellar light.

"What is going on down here?" she cried.

CHAPTER 5:

A Merry Christmas

"Look! Harold is dressed up like Santa Claus!" Toby shouted, rushing down the stairs.

"And Howie broke a lamp!" Pete said, following behind him.

Pete took the shade off Howie's head and scooped him up.

"That's the third time you've been bad this week!" he scolded. "This time the dogcatcher really will come and get you!"

"The dogcatcher?" asked Toby. "What are you talking about?"

"On Monday, Howie ate the last page of my mystery book," said Pete. "On Thursday, he broke my plastic skeleton that took me two months to put together. I told him if he didn't stop wrecking my stuff, the dogcatcher would come and carry him away in his bag."

"Poor Howie," said Mrs. Monroe, taking him from Pete's arms.

"No dogcatcher is going to get you. You can't help it if you break things sometimes. You're just a puppy. You still have a lot to learn."

"So this is where all the noise is coming from," Mr. Monroe said from the top of the stairs. "What do you think they're so excited about?"

"Christmas, I'll bet," Toby answered, giving me a pat. "Nobody can sleep before Christmas!"

"Well, I know someone who hasn't been sleeping," Mr. Monroe said with a grin.

Toby and Pete looked at each other and shouted, "Santa Claus!"

They flew up the stairs.

And Chester and I were right behind them.

"Just remember," Chester called. "I get to play with the ribbons!"

"Did Santa Claus bring all this stuff?" Howie asked when he saw the presents under the tree.

"Of course," I said. "That's what I was trying to tell you. Santa Claus carries presents in his bag—not naughty puppies."

Howie shook his head. "Mrs. Monroe was right, Uncle Harold. I do have a lot to learn."

"Oh well, you're not the only one,"
I said, glancing at Chester. He was all
tangled up in ribbon.

"What do you mean?" Chester cried.

"Nothing," I said, chuckling. "I'm just glad it's a merry Christmas—not a scary Christmas—after all!"